LA ISLA FANTÁSTICA

FANTASTIC ISLAND

Illustrated by Brenda Haw

Adapted from Puzzle Island, in the Usborne Young Puzzles series, by
Kathy Gemmell & Nicole Irving

Bilingual editor: Kate Needam
Design adaptation by John Russell

Language consultants:
Esther Lecumberri & Marta Nuñez

Original story by Susannah Leigh

Edited by Gaby Waters
Designed by Kim Blundell

Contents

2 **About this book**

4 **El puerto**
The port

6 **¿Qué isla?**
Which island?

8 **La búsqueda comienza**
The hunt begins

10 **El lago**
The lake

12 **En el bosque**
In the forest

14 **En el huerto**
In the orchard

16 **El Castillo Fantástico**
Fantastic Castle

18 **La guarida de los piratas**
The pirate's den

20 **El tesoro**
The treasure

22 **Answers**

23 **Word list and
pronunciation guide**

About this book

This book is about an apprentice pirate called Max, his pet parrot, Morgan, and their adventures on Fantastic Island. The story is in Spanish and English. You can look up the word list on page 23 if you want to check what any Spanish word means. This list also shows you how to say each Spanish word.

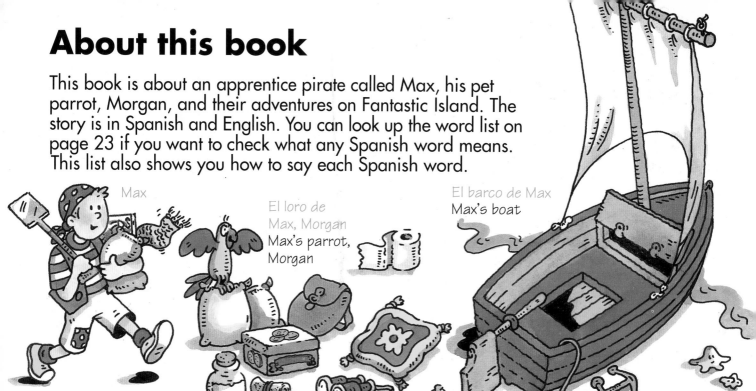

Max

El loro de
Max, Morgan
Max's parrot,
Morgan

El barco de Max
Max's boat

El equipo
para la aventura
Equipment for the adventure

La historia   The story

Para convertirse en un verdadero pirata, Max debe encontrar una insignia con una calavera.
To become a real pirate, Max must find a skull and crossbones badge.

La insignia con la calavera
Skull and crossbones badge

La insignia está escondida en el cofre del tesoro en algún lugar en el corazón de la Isla Fantástica.
The badge is hidden in the treasure chest somewhere at the heart of Fantastic Island.

El cofre del tesoro
Treasure chest

There is a puzzle on every double page.
Solve each one and help Max and Morgan on their way. All the Spanish words you need to solve the puzzles are in the word keys (look out for this sign: 🔑). If you get stuck, the answers are on page 22.

Things to look for

During his journey to the treasure chest, Max must collect the nine pieces of pirate kit shown here. One piece of the kit is hidden on every double page. Can you spot them all?

un sombrero de pirata
a pirate hat

un telescopio
a telescope

un sable
a cutlass

Para Max
For Max

un pendiente de oro
a gold earring

una botella de tónico fortalecedor
a bottle of fortifying tonic

una bota de pirata
a pirate boot

un garfio
a hook

un cepillo para loros
a parrot's brush

una bolsa de monedas de oro
a bag of gold coins

Horacio the Horrible

Horacio is a sneaky pirate desperate to beat Max to the treasure. See if you can spot him lurking on every double page.

Horacio

Pink elephants

Fantastic Island is home to the only remaining pink elephants in the world. There is at least one hiding on every double page. Can you find them all?

How to sound Spanish

Some letters sound different in Spanish. Here are a few tips to help you say the difficult ones.

You never say h, but the letter j is said like the "h" in "half". Ll is like the "y" in "yes", ñ is like the first "n" in "onion", qu is like the "c" in "cat" and v is like the "b" in "bad".

Y is like the "y" in yes, unless on its own, when it is like the "e" in "me". Z is like the "th" in "this" in north or central Spain, but

in southern Spain or South America it is like the "s" in "sat".

The Spanish r is rolled, it sounds a little like a dog growling. C and g only sound different when they come before "i" or "e". Then c is like z, (it sounds like "th" or "s", and g is like j, (it sounds like "h").

The signs ¿ and ¡ are used in written Spanish, to introduce a question or exclamation, as in ¿Qué isla? Which island? or ¡Qué raro! How strange!

3

El puerto The port

La aventura de Max empieza una mañana temprano.
Max's adventure starts early one morning.

Sale en su barquito rojo.
He sets off in his little red boat.

Dice adiós a sus padres, a su hermana y a su abuela.
He says goodbye to his parents, his sister and his grandma.

De repente, piensa en algo que le preocupa.
Suddenly, he thinks of something that worries him.

No sabe dónde está la Isla Fantástica.
He does not know where Fantastic Island is.

**Look at what people in the port are saying.
Can you spot what each of them can see?
Which person may be
able to help Max?**

Key	
adiós	goodbye
buen viaje	have a good journey
yo veo	I see
un faro	a lighthouse
una cometa	a kite
una bicicleta	a bicycle
una isla	an island
una sirena	a mermaid
una foca	a seal
un gato	a cat
un pañuelo	a handkerchief
un ancla	an anchor
no ... nada	nothing

4

¿Qué isla?   Which island?

Max llega en seguida a un pequeño grupo de islas.
Max soon arrives at a small group of islands.

Mira con sus prismáticos.
He looks through his binoculars.

Las islas se parecen mucho. "¿Cuál es la Isla Fantástica?"
se pregunta. De repente Morgan chilla: "¡Escucha!"
The islands all look the same. "Which one is Fantastic
Island?" he wonders. Suddenly Percival squawks: "Listen!"

"Oigo voces," dice Max, "y todas hablan de elefantes.
¡Qué raro!"
"I can hear voices," says Max, "and they're all talking
about elephants. How strange!"

**Can you tell which island is which from what
the animals are saying?**

Key 🗝️

en	on
la isla (de)	island
la manzana	apple
la cereza	cherry
la naranja	orange
la fresa	strawberry
la frambuesa	raspberry
fantástica	fantastic
hay	there is/there are
no hay	there are no
(el/los) elefante(s)	elephant(s)
un	one/a/an
dos	two
amarillo	yellow
rojo	red
rosa	pink
gris, grises	grey
violeta	purple
y	and

En la isla de la Manzana, hay un elefante gris.

En la isla de la Cereza, hay un elefante violeta y un elefante amarillo.

En la isla de la Naranja, no hay elefantes.

La búsqueda comienza
The hunt begins

¡Por fin tierra firme! Max ve un cartel y varios caminos que conducen a un bosque.
Dry land at last! Max sees a sign and several paths which lead into a forest.

Confundido, hace las dos cosas que están escritas en el cartel. De pronto, oye voces que le responden.
Puzzled, he does the two things written on the sign. At once, he hears voices answering him.

"¡Eso es!" exclama. "Ya sé qué debo hacer para encontrar el camino."
"That's it!" he exclaims. "Now I know what I have to do to find the right path."

Max must pass all the animals saying hello to reach the right path. Which way should he go?

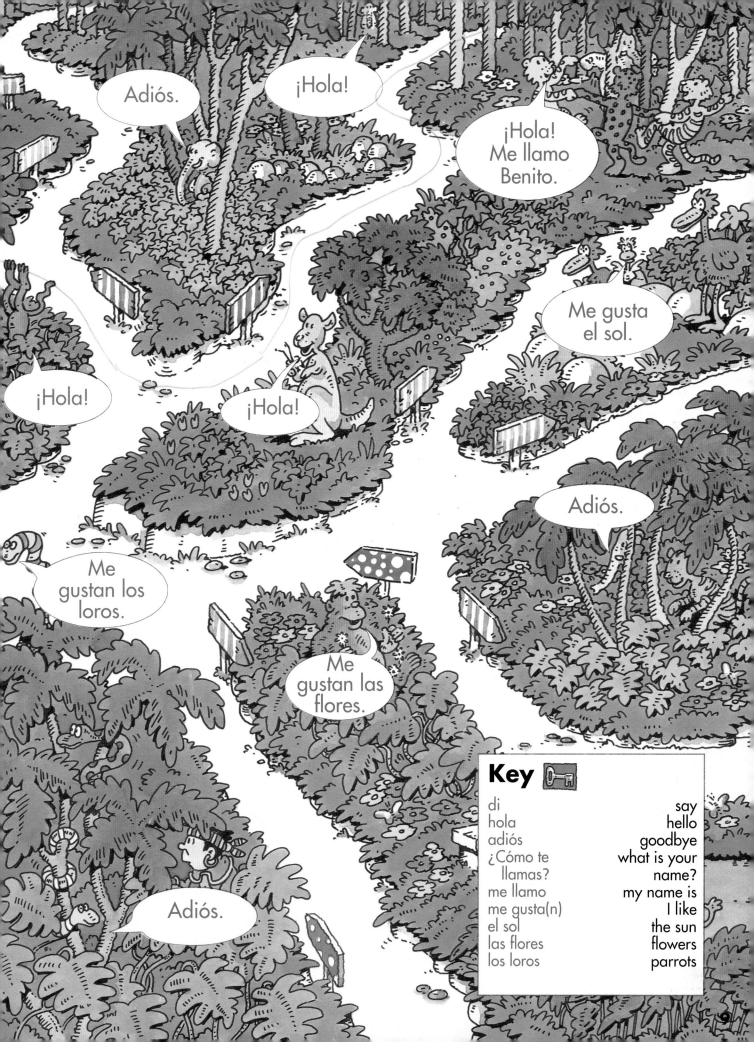

Key

di	say
hola	hello
adiós	goodbye
¿Cómo te llamas?	what is your name?
me llamo	my name is
me gusta(n)	I like
el sol	the sun
las flores	flowers
los loros	parrots

9

El lago   The lake

Max llega en seguida a un lago cubierto de hojas gigantes.
Max soon reaches a lake covered with giant leaves.

Decide cruzarlo saltando de hoja en hoja.
He decides to cross it by leaping from leaf to leaf.

Max descubre un cartel en medio del lago. El cartel dice
que debe seguir las hojas marcadas del uno al veinte.
Max spots a sign in the middle of the lake. The sign says
he must follow the leaves marked one to twenty.

Max mira alrededor desesperado. Todas las hojas parecen
numeradas. ¿Cuáles debe pisar para cruzar el lago?
Max looks around in despair. All the leaves seem to be
numbered. Which ones should he step on to cross the lake?

**Can you help Max count to twenty on the
leaves to find the right way across the lake?**

Key

sigue	follow
los números	the numbers
del	from
al	to
uno	one
dos	two
tres	three
cuatro	four
cinco	five
seis	six
siete	seven
ocho	eight
nueve	nine
diez	ten
once	eleven
doce	twelve
trece	thirteen
catorce	fourteen
quince	fifteen
dieciséis	sixteen
diecisiete	seventeen
dieciocho	eighteen
diecinueve	nineteen
veinte	twenty

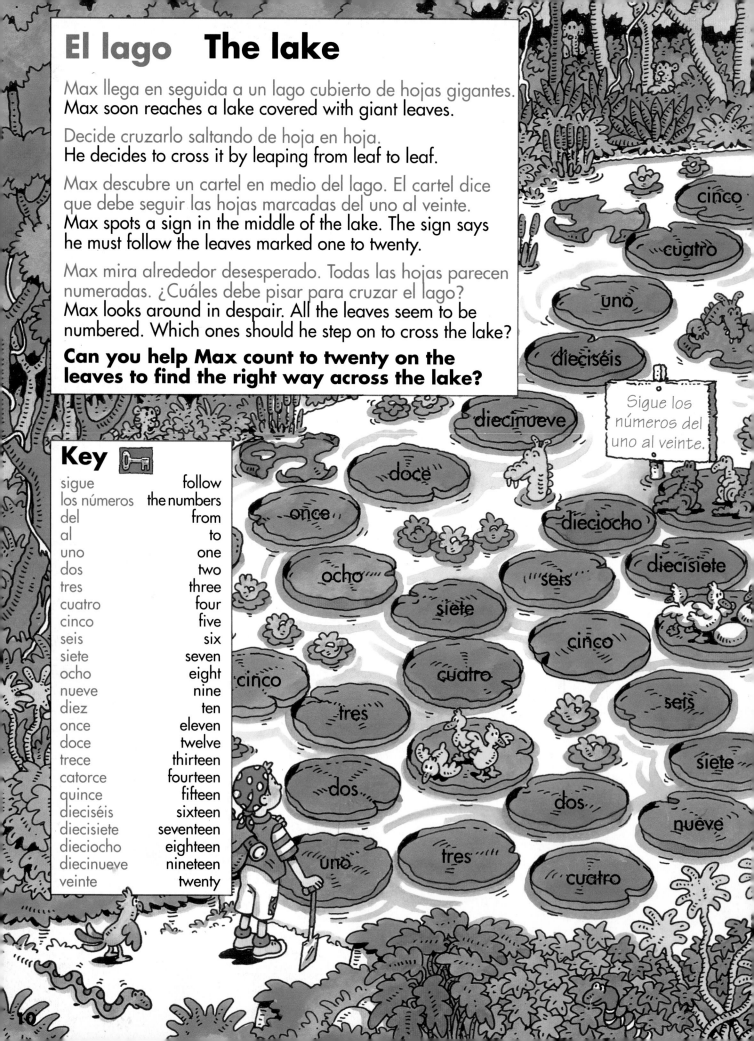

Sigue los números del uno al veinte.

En el bosque   In the forest

Al otro lado del lago, Max ve una cosa muy rara.
On the other side of the lake, Max sees something very odd.

Un hombre está mirando desde lo alto de una gran torre.
A man is watching from the top of a big tower.

"¡Hola!" grita Max. "¿Sabe usted dónde está el tesoro?"
"Hello!" shouts Max. "Do you know where the treasure is?"

"Sí," responde el hombre, "te lo diré, pero antes, ayúdame."
"Yes," answers the man, "I'll tell you, but first, help me."

"Estoy buscando los seis últimos animales de mi libro de
Animales Extraordinarios."
"I am looking for the last six animals in my book of
Amazing Animals."

**Can you spot all the animals the man
is looking for somewhere in the forest?**

Estoy buscando un
león, un tigre, una jirafa,
un mono, una serpiente
y un perro.

Silencio por favor.
No molestar.

Key 🔑

estoy buscando	I am looking for
no molestar	do not disturb
un león	a lion
un tigre	a tiger
una jirafa	a giraffe
un mono	a monkey
una serpiente	a snake
un perro	a dog
y	and
(el) silencio	silence
por favor	please

En el huerto In the orchard

El viejo le dice a Max en qué arbusto encontrará la siguiente pista.
The old man tells Max in which bush he will find the next clue.

Es una llave.
It is a key.

Where does the label on the key tell Max to go?

Cuando Max entra en el huerto, oye un ruido.
As Max enters the orchard, he hears a noise.

Un mono azul murmura algo.
A blue monkey is muttering something.

Should Max trust what the monkey says?

De repente, Horacio salta de detrás de un árbol.
Suddenly, Horacio leaps out from behind a tree.

Le pone a Max una red sobre la cabeza.
He puts a net over Max's head.

What is Horacio going to do?

14

Max se quita la red, pero Horacio ya ha desaparecido.
Max takes off the net, but Horacio has already disappeared.

Después oye más cuchicheos.
Then he hears more muttering.

Where does the statue tell Max to go?

¡Vete al Castillo Fantástico! No es amarillo. No es rojo.

Yo no miento nunca.

Max sale hacia el Castillo Fantástico. En seguida llega a un claro.
Max sets off for Fantastic Castle. He soon comes to a clearing.

Delante de él se levantan tres castillos.
In front of him stand three castles.

Can you use the statue's directions to answer Max's question for him?

Key 🗝

voy a	I am going
vete	go
yo miento	I lie
no … nunca	never
siempre	always
¿cuál es …?	which is…?
no es	it is not
encontrar	to find
el tesoro	the treasure
al	to the
(el) huerto	orchard
(el) castillo	castle
rojo	red
amarillo	yellow
antes que	before
tú	you

¿Cuál es el Castillo Fantástico?

15

El Castillo Fantástico   Fantastic Castle

Max llega al castillo azul.
La puerta está cerrada con llave.
Max arrives at the blue castle.
The gate is locked.

"Éste debe ser el Castillo Fantástico,"
suspira Max. "¿Pero cómo voy
a entrar?"

"This must be Fantastic Castle,"
sighs Max. "But how am I
going to get in?"

Necesito
una llave.

Tengo sed y quisiera
un chocolate.

Tengo
hambre. Quisiera
un pastel.

Max deja en el suelo su bolso que
pesa mucho. "Vamos a ver, tal vez
pueda encontrar algo útil en mi bolso."
Max puts down his heavy bag. "Let's see,
perhaps I can find something useful in my bag."

**Look at the contents of Max's bag. Can you find all the
things the weary adventurers need to keep them going?**

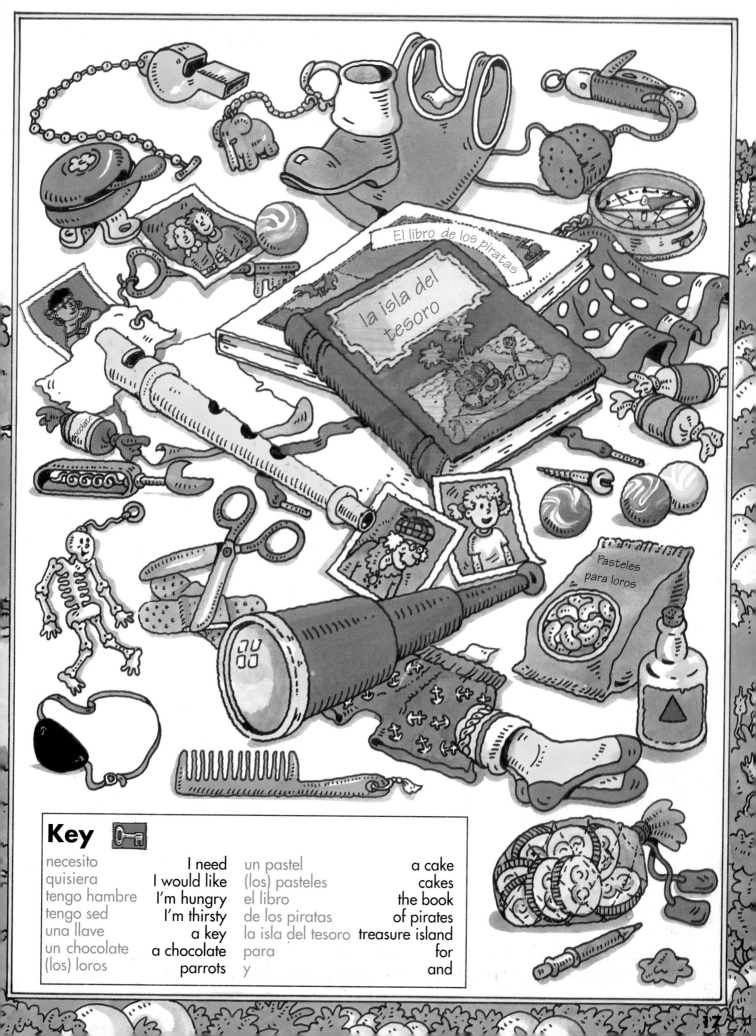

El libro de los piratas

la isla del tesoro

Pasteles para loros

Key 🔑

necesito	I need	un pastel	a cake
quisiera	I would like	(los) pasteles	cakes
tengo hambre	I'm hungry	el libro	the book
tengo sed	I'm thirsty	de los piratas	of pirates
una llave	a key	la isla del tesoro	treasure island
un chocolate	a chocolate	para	for
(los) loros	parrots	y	and

La guarida de los piratas
The pirate's den

La llave abre fácilmente la puerta. Max y los loros buscan por el castillo.

The key opens the gate easily. Max and the parrots search the castle.

Cuando entran en la última habitación, Max exclama, "¡Es la guarida de un pirata. Casi hemos llegado!"

As they enter the last room, Max exclaims, "This is a pirate's den. We're nearly there!"

"Pero ¿cuál es la puerta para encontrar el tesoro?"
"But which is the right door for the treasure?"

Los ratones del pirata quieren ayudarle. Por desgracia para Max, son un poco cortos de vista.

The pirate's mice want to help him. Unluckily for Max, they are a little near-sighted.

The correct door is the only one which fits one of the mice's descriptions. Which door is it?

Abre la puerta azul, anaranjada y negra.

Abre la puerta rosa, azul y verde.

Abre la puerta anaranjada y verde.

El tesoro The treasure

Max abre la puerta. Ve un camino y lo sigue hasta llegar a una enorme cascada.
Max opens the door. He sees a path and follows it to a huge waterfall.

"¡Mira!" grita a Morgan. "Una cruz en el suelo. Vamos a cavar aquí."
"Look!" he yells to Morgan. "A cross on the ground. Let's dig here."

Mientras está cavando, Max se da cuenta de que hay gente mirando.
As he digs, Max realizes that people are watching.

What are they all telling Max to do?

Key

de prisa	quick
date prisa	hurry up
estoy buscando	I am looking for
un reloj	a watch
una moto	a motorcycle
un coche	a car
una pelota	a ball
una peluca	a wig
una insignia	a badge
una calavera	a skull
(los) patines	roller skates
unos	some
con	with

De repente, la pala de Max golpea algo duro.
¡El cofre del tesoro!
Suddenly, Max's spade hits something hard.
The treasure chest!

Todo el mundo se apresura para ayudar a Max a
sacar el cofre.
Everyone hurries to help Max lift out the chest.

Max salta de alegría. Por fin es un verdadero pirata y
además tiene muchos nuevos amigos.
Max leaps for joy. At last he is a real pirate
and he has lots of new friends as well.

**Can you spot all the things that Max
and his new friends are looking for?**

Answers

Pages 4-5
The objects that people can see are circled. This lookout may be able to help Max.

Pages 6-7
Here you can see which island is which.

La isla de la Frambuesa

La isla Fantástica

La isla de la Manzana

La isla de la Naranja

La isla de la Cereza

La isla de la Fresa

Pages 8-9
The path Max should take is shown in black.

Pages 10-11
The leaves Max should step on are shown by the black line.

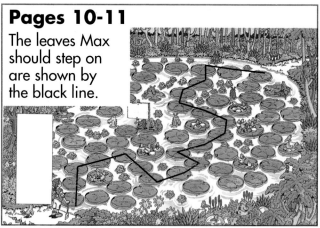

Pages 12-13
The animals the old man is looking for are circled.

Pages 14-15
The label tells Max to go to the orchard. He should not trust what the monkey says because the monkey always lies. Horacio says he is going to find the treasure before Max. The statue tells Max to go to Fantastic Castle. Fantastic Castle is the blue castle.

Pages 16-17
The things Max and the parrots need are circled.

Pages 18-19
This is the correct door.

This mouse gives the right description.

Pages 20-21
Everyone is telling Max to hurry up. The things that Max and his new friends are looking for are circled.

Did you spot everything?

Pages	Pink elephants	Equipment
4-5	two	pirate boot
6-7	one	fortifying juice
8-9	six	telescope
10-11	two	gold earring
12-13	three	hook
14-15	two	gold coins
16-17	three	parrot's brush
18-19	two	cutlass
20-21	three	pirate hat

Did you remember to find Horacio? Look back and spot him on every double page.

Word list and pronunciation guide

Here is a list of all the Spanish words and phrases used in this book. All the naming words (nouns) have el, la, los or las before them. These all mean "the". Spanish nouns are either masculine or feminine. You use el and los with masculine nouns, and la and las with feminine nouns. When you see los or las, it means the noun is plural (more than one).

Spanish describing words (adjectives) ending in o change to a when they describe feminine nouns. Here, the masculine version is written first, followed by /a, for example rojo/a (red). When an adjective describes a plural noun, it usually has an s after the o or a, for example las flores rojas (red flowers).

Each Spanish word in this list has its pronunciation shown after it (in letters like this). Read these letters as if they were English words. The ones that are underlined should be said slightly louder than the rest. In South America or southern Spain, the "th" sound shown here is pronounced as "ss". For more about how to say Spanish words, see page 3.

Spanish	Pronunciation	English
a	a	to OR at
abre	abray	open OR (he/she) opens
la abuela	la abwella	grandmother
además	ademass	as well
adiós	adeeyoss	goodbye
¡ajá!	aha	ha! ha!
al	al	to the
la alegría	la alegreeya	joy
algo	algo	something
algún, alguna	algoon, algoona	some
alrededor	alrededor	around
amarillo/a	amareelyo/a	yellow
el amigo, la amiga	el ameego, la ameega	friend (boy, girl)
anaranjado/a	anaranhado/a	orange
el ancla	el ankla	anchor
los animales	loss aneemaless	animals
antes	antess	before OR first
aquí	akee	here
el árbol	el arbol	tree
el arbusto	el arboosto	bush
la aventura	la abentoora	adventure
ayúdame	ayoodamay	help me
ayudar	ayoodar	to help
azul	athool	blue
el barco	el barko	boat
el barquito	el barkeeto	little boat
la bicicleta	la beetheekleta	bike
blanco/a	blanko/a	white
la bolsa	la bolsa	bag
el bolso	el bolso	bag OR handbag
el bosque	el bosskay	forest
la bota	la bota	boot
la botella	la botelya	bottle
buen viaje	bwen bee-a-hay	have a good journey
buscan	boosskan	(they) search
buscando	boosskando	looking for
buscar	boosskar	to search OR look for
la búsqueda	la boossketha	hunt OR search
la cabeza	la kabetha	head
la calavera	la kalabaira	skull (and crossbones)
el camino	el kameeno	path
el cartel	el kartel	sign
la cascada	la kasskada	waterfall
casi	kassee	almost OR nearly
el castillo	el kassteelyo	castle
catorce	katorthay	fourteen
cavando	kabando	digging
cavar	kabar	to dig
el cepillo	el thepeelyo	brush
la cereza	la theretha	cherry
cerrado/a	therrado/a	closed
chilla	cheelya	(he/she) squawks
el chocolate	el chokolatay	chocolate
cinco	theenko	five
el claro	el klaro	clearing
el coche	el kochay	car
el cofre	el kofray	chest
la cometa	la kometa	kite
comienza	komeeyentha	(he/she/it) begins
¿cómo?	komo	how?
¿cómo te llamas?	komo tay lyamass	what is your name?
con	kon	with
conducen	kondoothen	(they) lead
confundido/a	konfoondeedo/a	puzzled
convertirse en	konbairteerssay en	to become
el corazón	el korathon	heart
cortos de vista	kortoss day beessta	near-sighted
la cosa	la kossa	thing
la cruz	la krooth	cross
cruzar	kroothar	to cross
¿cuál?	kwal	which (one)?
¿cuáles?	kwaless	which (ones)?
cuando	kwando	when
cuatro	kwatro	four
cubierto/a	koobeeyairto/a	covered
los cuchicheos	loss koocheechayoss	muttering
date prisa	datay preessa	hurry up
de	day	of OR from
de prisa	day preessa	quickly
de pronto	day pronto	at once
de repente	day repentay	suddenly
debe	debay	(he/she) must
debo	debo	I must
decide	detheeday	(he/she) decides
deja	deha	(he/she) leaves
del	del	of the OR from
delante de	daylantay day	in front of
desaparecido	dessaparetheedo	disappeared
descubre	desskoobray	(he/she) discovers OR spots
desde lo alto	dezday lo alto	from the top
desesperado	dessessperado	in despair
después	desspwess	after OR then
detrás de	detrass day	behind

23

Spanish	Pronunciation	English
di	dee	say
dice	deethay	(he/she) says
diecinueve	dee-ethee-nwebay	nineteen
dieciocho	dee-ethee-ocho	eighteen
dieciséis	dee-ethee-sayss	sixteen
diecisiete	dee-ethee-see-etay	seventeen
diez	dee-eth	ten
diré	deeray	I will say
doce	dothay	twelve
¿dónde?	donday	where?
dos	doss	two
duro	dooro	hard
el	el	the
él	el	he OR him
el elefante	el elefantay	elephant
empieza	empee-etha	(he/she/it) starts
en	en	in OR on
en seguida	en segeeda	soon OR right away
encontrar	enkontrar	to find
encontrará	enkontrara	(he/she) will find
enorme	enormay	huge
entra	entra	(he/she) enters
entrar	entrar	to enter
el equipo	el ekeepo	equipment
es	ess	(he/she/it) is
escondido/a	esskondeedo/a	hidden
escrito/a	esskreeto/a	written
escucha	esskoocha	listen OR (he/she) listens
eso	esso	that
está	essta	(he/she/it) is
están	esstan	(they) are
éste	esstay	this
estoy	esstoy	I am
exclama	exklama	(he/she) exclaims
extraordinario/a(s)	extra-ordeenaree-o/a(ss)	amazing OR extraordinary
fácilmente	fatheelmentay	easily
fantástico/a	fantassteeko/a	fantastic
el faro	el faro	lighthouse
las flores	lass floress	flowers
la foca	la foka	seal
fortalecedor/a	fortalethedor/a	fortifying
la frambuesa	la frambwessa	raspberry
la fresa	la fressa	strawberry
el garfio	el garfee-o	hook
el gato	el gato	cat
la gente	la hentay	people
gigante(s)	heegante(ss)	giant
golpea	golpaya	(he/she) hits
gran	gran	big
gris, grises	greess, greessess	grey
grita	greeta	(he/she) yells
el grupo	el groopo	group
la guarida	la gwareeda	den
ha	a	(he/she/it) has ...
la habitación	la abeetatheeyon	room
hablan	ablan	(they) talk
hace	athay	(he/she) makes OR (he/she) does
hacer	athair	to make OR to do
hacia	athee-a	toward OR for
hasta	asta	until OR to
hay	eye	there is OR there are
hemos	emoss	we have ...
la hermana	la airmana	sister
la historia	la eesstoree-a	story
la hoja	la oha	leaf
hola	ola	hello OR hi
el hombre	el ombray	man
el huerto	el wairto	orchard
la insignia	la eensseegnee-a	badge
la isla	la eessla	island
la jirafa	la heerafa	giraffe
el lado	el lado	side
el lago	el lago	lake
le	lay	to him OR to her
el león	el layon	lion
el libro	el leebro	book
la llave	la lyabay	key
llega	lyega	(he/she) arrives (at OR reaches
llegado	lyegado	arrived
llegar	lyegar	to arrive
el loro	el loro	parrot
el lugar	el loogar	place
la mañana	la manyana	morning
la manzana	la manthana	apple
marcado/a(s)	markado/a(ss)	marked
más	mass	more
me gusta(n)	may goossta(n)	I like
me llamo	may lyamo	my name is
medio	medee-o	middle
mi	mee	my
miento	mee-ento	I lie
mientras	mee-entrass	while OR as
mira	meera	look OR (he/she/it) looks
mirando	meerando	looking OR watching
las monedas	lass monedass	coins
el mono	el mono	monkey
la moto	la moto	motorcycle
mucho/a(s)	moocho/a(ss)	much OR many
murmura	moormoora	(he/she) mutters
muy	mooy	very
la naranja	la naranha	orange
necesito	nethesseeto	I need
negro/a	negro/a	black
no ... nada	no ... nada	nothing
no ... nunca	no ... noonka	never
no es	no ess	(he/she/it) is not
no hay	no eye	there is/are not
no molestar	no molesstar	do not disturb
no sabe	no sabay	(he/she) doesn't know
nueve	nwebay	nine
numerado/a(s)	noomerado/a(ss)	numbered
los números	noomeross	numbers
ocho	ocho	eight
oigo	oygo	I hear
once	onthay	eleven
oro	oro	gold
otro/a	otro/a	other
oye	oyay	(he/she) hears
los padres	loss padress	parents

Spanish	Pronunciation	English
la pala	la *pala*	spade
el pañuelo	el *pan-ywelo*	handkerchief
para	*para*	for OR to
parecen	par*ethen*	(they) seem
el pastel	el *passtel*	cake
los patines	loss pat*eeness*	roller skates
la pelota	la pe*lota*	ball
la peluca	la pe*looka*	wig
el pendiente	el pendee*yentay*	earring
pequeño/a	pe*kenyo/a*	small
pero	*pero*	but
perro	*perro*	dog
pesa	*pessa*	(he/she/it) weighs
piensa	pee-*enssa*	(he/she) thinks
el pirata	el *peerata*	pirate
pisar	pee*ssar*	to step on
la pista	la *peessta*	clue
poco	*poko*	little
pone	*ponay*	(he/she) puts
por desgracia	por dess*grathee-a*	unluckily
por favor	por *fabor*	please
por fin	por *feen*	at last
preocupa	prayo*koopa*	(he/she/it) worries
los prismáticos	loss preess*mateekoss*	binoculars
pueda	*pweda*	I might be able to
la puerta	la *pwairta*	door OR gate
el puerto	el *pwairto*	port
que	*kay*	that
¿qué?	*kay*	what? OR which?
¡qué raro!	*kay* raro	how strange!
quieren	kee-*eren*	(they) want
quince	*keenthay*	fifteen
quisiera	keessee-*aira*	I would like
raro/a	*raro/a*	strange OR odd
los ratones	loss ra*toness*	mice
la red	la *red*	net
el reloj	el re*loh*	watch
responde	ress*ponday*	(he/she) answers
responden	ress*ponden*	(they) answer
rojo/a	*roho/a*	red
rosa	*rossa*	pink
el ruido	el roo-*eedo*	noise
sabe	*sabay*	(he/she) knows
¿sabe usted?	*sabay* ooss*ted*	do you know?
el sable	el *sablay*	cutlass
sacar	sa*kar*	to take out
sale	*salay*	(he/she) sets off
salta	*salta*	(he/she) leaps (out)
saltando	sal*tando*	leaping
sé	*say*	I know
se apresura	say apress*oora*	(he/she) hurries
se da cuenta de	say da *kwenta* day	(he/she) realizes
seguir	se*geer*	to follow
seis	*sayss*	six
se levantan	say le*bantan*	(they) stand
se parecen	say par*ethen*	(they) look alike

Spanish	Pronunciation	English
se pregunta	say pre*goonta*	(he/she) wonders
se quita	say *keeta*	(he/she) takes off
ser	*sair*	to be
la serpiente	la *sairpee-entay*	snake
sí	*see*	yes
siempre	see-*empray*	always
siete	see-*etay*	seven
sigue	*seegay*	(he/she/it) follows
siguiente	seegee-*entay*	next OR following
el silencio	el *seelenthee-o*	silence
la sirena	la *seerena*	mermaid
sobre	*sobray*	on
el sol	el *sol*	sun
el sombrero	el som*brairo*	hat
son	*son*	(they) are
su, sus	*soo, sooss*	his OR her
el suelo	el *swelo*	floor OR ground
suspira	sooss*peera*	(he/she) sighs
tal vez	*tal beth*	perhaps
te	*tay*	to you
el telescopio	el teless*kopee-o*	telescope
temprano	tem*prano*	early
tengo hambre	*tengo ambray*	I'm hungry
tengo sed	*tengo sed*	I'm thirsty
el tesoro	el *tessoro*	treasure
tiene	tee-*enay*	(he/she/it) has
la tierra firme	la tee-*erra feermay*	dry land
el tigre	el *teegray*	tiger
todos/as	*todoss/ass*	all OR everyone
todo el mundo	*todo* el *moondo*	everyone
el tónico	el *toneeko*	tonic
la torre	la *torray*	tower
trece	*trethay*	thirteen
tres	*tress*	three
tú	*too*	you
último/a	*oolteemo/a*	last
un, uno, una	*oon, oono, oona*	one OR a
unos, unas	*oonoss, oonass*	some
útil	*ooteel*	useful
vamos a …	*bamoss a …*	let's …
varios/as	*baree-oss/ass*	several
ve	*bay*	(he/she) sees
veinte	*bayntay*	twenty
veo	*bay-o*	I see
ver	*bair*	to see
verdadero/a	*bairdadairo/a*	real OR true
verde	*bairday*	green
vete	*betay*	go
el viejo	el bee-*eho*	old man
violeta	bee-*oleta*	purple
las voces	lass *bothess*	voices
voy	*boy*	I am going OR I go
y	*ee*	and
ya	*ya*	already OR now
yo	*yo*	I